heels of his feet.

He ran past the pizza place, past the newsstand on the corner and past the local elementary school. Two boys sat on a step, hunched over a video game. When Izzy entered the park, he saw kids playing hopscotch. Guys hooted from the basketball court. For a split second, Izzy thought about joining the game. Then he remembered: there was no time. Izzy wasn't just dashing through the neighbourhood for kicks. He was on a training run.

That's because Izzy was Izzy Daniels, teen boxing sensation, son of former Golden Gloves champion Kenneth Daniels. Izzy's dad was the owner of Daniels Gym and Izzy's personal coach. Not only did Izzy have the makings of a champ; he had the birthright, too.

If Izzy didn't have time for hoops, he definitely didn't have time to hassle his neighbour Mary Thomas. But all of a sudden, there she was, smack-bang in the middle of the playground. She was playing Double Dutch with

2

her friends Shauna and Keisha. She had a look of agonized concentration on her face. Then again, maybe she'd just spied Izzy. She never looked happy to see him.

Izzy needed to keep going. He couldn't lose momentum. But something kept him standing there. He watched the ropes whirl eggbeater style around and around.

"Keisha, loose it, loose it," he heard Mary demand.

"It is loose," Keisha shot back.

"It's got to hit the street." Mary sounded frustrated.

"Smoke it!" shouted another voice. Izzy hadn't seen Yolanda Brooks at first, but he couldn't help hearing her sharp, angry voice. She was even bossier than Mary.

Izzy watched the ropes speed up. They looked cool when they went that fast, dizzying, even. He had every intention of turning around, continuing his run. Instead, he grinned devilishly to himself and leaped in.

CHAPTER ONE

Brooklyn: home to Prospect Park and Coney Island; the birthplace of Junior's cheesecake, Nathan's hot dogs and countless hip-hop stars.

It was for these reasons and many others that Izzy – short for Isadore – couldn't imagine living anywhere else. As he bounded out of Daniels Gym, the smells of the street – the guava pastries from the bakery, the guy selling tacos from a truck – wafted up his nose and invigorated him. He turned up his MP3 player and ran harder. Through his boxing shoes, he could feel the hard pavement pulsate on the

JUMP IN!

Book of the Film

Adapted by M. C. King

Based on the Disney Channel Original Movie, *Jump In!*

Written by Doreen Spicer and Regina Hicks and Karin Gist

First published by Parragon in 2007
Parragon
Queen Street House
4 Queen Street
Bath BA1 1HE, UK

ISBN 978-1-4075-0448-3

Printed in UK

Bath · New York · Singapore · Hong Kong · Cologne · Delhi · Melbourne

He stood facing Mary as the ropes sagged and tangled around them. *Score*!

"Izzy!" Mary shouted.

"Mary!" Izzy imitated Mary's irritated tone.

"Get out!" Mary commanded.

Izzy couldn't help it. He was enjoying himself. "Make me," he teased.

"Why do you always have to mess with us?" Mary asked.

Well, that was a no-brainer. "Uh . . . 'cause it's fun," Izzy replied.

"Well, leave," Mary demanded. "We gotta practise."

Izzy wondered if Mary had conked her head on the pavement or something. Practise? Why was she taking this little playground game seriously?

"For what?" he baulked. "Double Dutch? Puh-leeze."

Yolanda explained. "The regional competition is this Friday. And our routine has to be tight if we want to get to city."

Izzy didn't know what that meant. City? What was that? And there was a regional competition for skipping? Next thing you knew, there'd be competitions for pick-up sticks or jacks. He looked at the girls' serious faces and tried not to laugh.

"Just turn the rope and jump," he said. "It ain't rocket science."

Mary looked offended. "Whatever," she scoffed. "Go."

If there was one thing Izzy could say about Mary, it was this: the girl was a fighter. Seeing as he was one too, Izzy had to respect that. But of course, he wouldn't let Mary know that. Instead, he purposely but gently bumped into her so their shoulders touched. He knew that move would get on her nerves, and that was just what Izzy wanted.

The smell hit him as soon as he entered the house. It smelled tangy and burning at once, and Izzy knew immediately: his father was cooking.

Ever since Izzy's mum had died, Mr Daniels had done everything he could to recreate the cosy home life they used to enjoy. Izzy appreciated the efforts, especially because his little sister, Karin, was still in need of lots of hands-on attention.

Izzy followed the sound of voices into the kitchen. His dad was standing over the stove, stirring the stinky mystery concoction. Karin was sitting at the table. She looked up when she saw Izzy.

"Dad's famous chilli," she said, looking fearful.

Mr Daniels had his back to his kids, and couldn't see the looks they exchanged. "With extra peppers," he announced. "Just the way you like it, right Izzy?"

"Right, Dad," Izzy answered with a wink to his sister. They were experts at silent communication, and Izzy mouthed: "I'll make you something later."

Mr Daniels ladled the chilli, if you could call it that, into individual bowls.

"Stuck out for a longer workout tonight?" he said to Izzy. "That a boy."

Izzy nodded. He could have admitted he'd spent the last part of his training run messing with Mary and her friends. Karin would have enjoyed hearing about the older girls. But Izzy stopped himself. When his dad thought Izzy was working hard at boxing, it made him happy. Why ruin that? Things were sad enough already.

CHAPTER TWO

Daniels Gym wasn't the biggest training facility in Brooklyn. It wasn't the most high-tech, either. But what it lacked in size and gear, it made up for in character and history. The walls were covered with old photos of former champs who'd trained there. Izzy often found himself staring at the pictures, imagining one of himself among them. He'd be posing like the one of his dad, holding up a Golden Gloves champion belt.

Izzy's best friends were Chuck and Lil' Earl. They weren't boxing prodigies like Izzy, but as Mr Daniels liked to say, boxing was "20 per cent talent, 80 per cent heart." Izzy's friends were all heart.

Chuck and Lil' Earl were sparring in the ring, under Mr Daniels's supervision, when Izzy entered the gym.

"Keep moving. That's it. Anticipate the moves," Mr Daniels coached. Izzy watched as Chuck scored an easy point off Lil' Earl. "Keep your gloves up, man," Mr Daniels told Lil' Earl. "Don't be so open."

But Lil' Earl couldn't help himself. He was all over the place. And when he saw Izzy coming, he lost his concentration entirely.

"Hey, Izzy!" he shouted.

He made a sad attempt at some fancy foot-work and ended up falling over his feet. Mr Daniels told them to take a breather.

Izzy could always tell when his dad had news. His lips curled up and his eyes flashed. As Izzy approached his dad, he steadied him-self in preparation. What was going on?

Thankfully, Mr Daniels didn't keep him

guessing for too long.

"So, Izzy," he said. "You want the good news or the good news?"

Izzy looked at his dad expectantly. Good news or good news? That could only mean one thing. "I'm going to the Golden Gloves?" he asked excitedly.

In his head, the picture of himself holding up a championship belt grew more and more in focus.

"Almost," his dad told him. "I got you an exhibition match, and if you win this one, you'll be ready."

An exhibition match. That was almost as good as going to the Golden Gloves.

"You know it," hooted Izzy. "So who am I up against?"

"The only other undefeated kid in the gym," his dad answered.

The picture of himself holding up the belt started to blur. Did his dad really mean who Izzy thought he meant? "Rodney?" he asked, even though he knew the answer. Rodney was Rodney Tyler, otherwise known as 'Big Rodney', the school's biggest bully and Izzy's fiercest opponent.

Rodney Tyler: the one thing standing between him and the Golden Gloves. Could he do it? Beat Big Rodney in an exhibition match? Apparently his dad thought so. Izzy may have still been processing the news, but Mr Daniels was already bursting with triumphant pride.

"Wow," he said, shaking his head in wonder. "The third generation of Daniels to win the Golden Gloves. You keep working on your stamina, winning your bouts, keeping your head in it, you can almost guarantee yourself a future in boxing. I couldn't, but you can."

Izzy needed his dad to slow down. He needed a moment to catch his breath. But there was no time for that. As of this moment, he was officially in training.

Felix was what you call an old-timer. He

was the kind of trainer you saw in old boxing movies like *Rocky* and *The Champ*. He'd worked at the gym for as long as anyone could remember. He may not have been as agile as he used to be, but he was still Izzy's favourite partner in the ring.

Izzy and Felix faced off as Izzy's dad watched from the sidelines. Izzy jabbed left and right. This was his first official practice before the match, and he needed to be serious. Except he couldn't help having fun. Felix threw a right hook. Izzy ducked. "Watch out now!" he warned. Out of the corner of his eye, he saw Chuck and Lil' Earl watching. For Lil' Earl's benefit, he stepped up the fancy footwork.

"Stop playing around," his dad scolded. "Stay focused! Let me see those combinations!"

Izzy jabbed to the right then served Felix with a quick uppercut.

"That's it," Mr Daniels encouraged. "Stay with it. Stay with him."

Izzy danced around the ring.

"How ya like me now?" he cried, turning to face his friends.

Maybe he was having too much fun. Because at that moment, Felix's left glove made contact with the side of Izzy's head gear. Okay, he'd barely hit him, but Izzy still was taken aback.

"Man, Felix, you hit me."

Felix shrugged. "You left yourself open."

"You were so busy trying to showboat," Izzy's dad told him.

Just earlier, his dad had been heralding him as the next champ. Now he had to be humble?!

"Ain't nothing wrong with being proud," Izzy said with a smirk.

"You're right." Mr Daniels smiled at his son. "But next time you're feeling proud, remember to keep your hands up."

Izzy would have to keep that in mind for tomorrow. Practice was over for now. His dad's next pupil, Tammy Lewis, one of the gym's only female boxers, had arrived. Izzy didn't know how Tammy dealt with it every day: she could not enter the gym without being teased. Izzy thought she was a glutton for punishment, because now as Lil' Earl teased her – was she here for ballet classes? he wanted to know – she just smirked. He watched as Tammy then ignored his pal and headed for the punchbag. Why did she put up with it?

That night, Izzy was getting ready for bed when he saw a light blazing from the window across the alley. He could see Mary Thomas's bedroom from his window. Usually the shades were drawn, but tonight they were up and the window was open. He peered in.

Unlike Izzy's room, Mary's was super-neat. Everything had a place. Izzy could practically see the floors gleaming from across the way. *What a control freak*, he thought, grinning. He looked a little closer. There, amidst the neatness, was Mary – and she was jumping! It took

Izzy a couple of seconds to put two and two together. There, in the dark of night, when she could have been watching TV or chilling out to music, Mary was practising Double Dutch!

Was this girl for real? Clearly, she was doing it to prove something to him. Izzy couldn't help but call her on it. He opened his window, leaned his head into the darkness, and hollered: "If you are trying to impress me, you're going to be up all night."

Mid-routine, Mary scowled, then slammed her window shut. The bang resonated across the alleyway. For some reason, the angry sound made Izzy smile.

CHAPTER THREE

≈

Izzy always missed his mum. But some times were worse than others.

The next morning, Izzy arrived in the kitchen to find a desperate scenario: Mr Daniels was attempting to do Karin's hair, but it wasn't working out very well. Izzy's poor little sister!

"How's that, baby?" Mr Daniels asked his daughter. Izzy cringed as his dad handed Karin a mirror. Her hair was a mess. If he were in his sister's place, he would have flipped a lid. But Karin was more patient than that. She gazed in the mirror and forced a smile. "Uh, nice,

Daddy," she stuttered.

The phone rang. "I'd better get that," said Mr Daniels, leaving Izzy and Karin alone.

"Slammin' hair," Izzy said, then chuckled.

"It's not funny," Karin said with a groan. "Help me."

Izzy was no expert at styling girls' hair, but he was better than his dad.

"Can you do it like Mummy used to?" Karin asked.

Izzy pulled the brush through his sister's hair. It snagged on a massive tangle.

"You miss her, huh?" he said, trying to be gentle.

"Yeah," she said.

"I know," said Izzy, working out the knot. "So do I."

Mr Daniels came back into the room. "There's a leak down at the gym," he said. "I've got to get down there."

Karin jerked her head up just as Izzy was working the mess into a ponytail.

"But what about the Double Dutch competition?" she cried.

The Double Dutch competition? Izzy wondered. As in Mary's Double Dutch competition?

"Don't worry," said Mr Daniels. "Izzy will take you."

Now Izzy looked alarmed. "Huh?" he baulked. But what about practice? The Golden Gloves? Whose side was his dad on?

"Mary will be there," sang Karin in a typically obnoxious eight-year-old-girl way.

Izzy knew that his little sister was clever, but could she read his mind?

Izzy could have been doing something important. He *could* have been doing homework. He *could* have been training. He could have been doing *anything* but this.

He stood on the stoop of their house, grinding his heel into the ground, and screamed for the eight millionth time: "Come on, Karin! Let's go!"

He'd already done her hair. What was taking the girl so long? She was only eight. It's not like she wore makeup or anything.

"Yo, Izzy." Izzy turned to see Chuck and Lil' Earl coming up the block. "You coming to the movies?" Chuck asked.

"It's free popcorn 'til five," Lil' Earl said.

Izzy shook his head mournfully. "I can't," he answered. "I gotta take Karin to some Double Dutch thing."

His friends looked horrified. "Yo, that's messed up," said Chuck.

Lil' Earl couldn't let an opportunity to say something smart go by. "Don't you need a cute little headband to get in?" he teased.

Izzy heaved a sigh of relief when, at last, Karin appeared.

The Double Dutch competition was in New York City's Harlem neighbourhood, an hour's train ride from Brooklyn. Walking alongside Izzy were four of Karin's little friends. This was a not-so-happy surprise for Izzy. He'd barely agreed to take Karin to this thing, let alone a bunch of her giggling gal pals. And not only did he have to hang out with them, he had to *pay* for them. They looked hungry!

At least he had his own buddies with him. Chuck and Lil' Earl were going to the movies uptown. It was a good thing, because who did they run into as soon as they exited the subway but Rodney? Not that Izzy *needed* backup. Still, it didn't hurt to have your buddies with you when you unexpectedly met your enemy.

Rodney stood there, towering over a much smaller boy. A few of his friends egged him on from the sidelines. Rodney had a basketball in his hands and he held it over the boy's head.

"Come and get it," he bellowed.

Could Rodney have picked an easier target? Izzy could have ignored the situation, but the boy's look of fright and misery left him no choice. "Yo, Rodney," he called. "Leave him alone."

Rodney turned and glared. "I know you're

not talking to me, loser."

Izzy didn't say anything. Rodney grimaced and dropped the ball. The boy scrambled for it and then ran off.

"I hear you're my competition in the exhibition match," Rodney said to Izzy.

"Looks that way," Izzy shot back.

"You'll never outbox me, daddy's boy."

Chuck interrupted. "Yes, he will. He's got mad skills."

Lil' Earl jumped in next. "That's right," he said, forcing his chest out. "He's been training. So you'd better watch out."

Rodney stepped towards Lil' Earl, who hopped back in fright. Rodney sniggered.

"Training?" he mocked. "Ooh, I'm scared. See you in the ring, loser."

After this confrontation, Izzy wanted to go to the Double Dutch competition even less. But when Chuck asked if he was sure about the movies, he had no choice but to say "Sorry, man."

He couldn't disappoint his sister.

CHAPTER FOUR

So there really was such a thing as Double Dutch city regionals? Izzy entered the large auditorium, saw the enormous welcome sign stretching across the wall and couldn't help being a little impressed.

The place was packed with jumpers of all shapes and sizes. There was a section for judges; one for jump counters. (Jump counters? Wow, people sure took this stuff seriously!) There was even a local news crew interviewing some contestants. Izzy recognized the sports reporter; she covered boxing sometimes.

And everyone was, no pun intended, *jumpy*. Every face that Izzy laid eyes on looked contorted and tense: the mum inspecting her daughter's makeup, the judge measuring a rope for accuracy, the team members practising in jittery clumps and looking furtively around as they sized up the competition.

Karin tugged on Izzy's sleeve. "Come on," she said, and motioned to the other side of the room where Mary's team, the Joy Jumpers, was practising. Izzy followed reluctantly as Karin and her friends ran ahead. He walked slowly, taking his time so that anyone who saw him would know he wasn't in a rush.

The Joy Jumpers were doing some stretching exercises.

"You guys are the bomb!" Karin gushed.

"Let's hope the judges think so," Yolanda, the newest member of the team, responded drily.

Mary looked Izzy up and down. "Izzy Daniels at a Double Dutch competition? What happened? You lose a bet?"

Izzy was cooking up something witty to say back. He didn't want Mary to think he'd come there just to see her. But before he had a chance to smart-mouth her back, the Dutch Dragons showed up. At least Izzy knew they were the Dutch Dragons from the team name spelled out across their T-shirts.

A girl named Gina got right in Mary's face.

"Hey, Mary. We heard you guys couldn't find a fourth this year, so you guys retired."

Mary turned her attention away from Izzy.

"You heard wrong, Gina," she snapped.

Mary's friend Keisha could be a big-mouth.

"Yeah, 'cause Yolanda moved here from Atlanta, and she's good. Really good. So you Dutch Dragons better watch out because—"

Mary glared at Keisha with a 'Shut up, shut up, shut up' look on her face. Keisha stopped talking.

"We are so scared," Gina mocked. She and the Dutch Dragons walked off.

"Who was that?" Yolanda asked.

Mary explained that the Dutch Dragons were last year's regional champs.

"They're good," Keisha said, shaking her head.

"So are you guys!" said Karin, who couldn't help but try to pump the Joy Jumpers up.

Mary grumbled that if they just stood there chatting, they wouldn't have a chance of qualifying. And so Izzy, Karin and her friends went to find their seats. Izzy was pretty sure he could feel Mary's eyes on him as he walked away.

"Joy Jumpers, Dutch Dragons and Soul Steppers, please take the floor," announced the MC. Izzy watched as the teams walked to face the judges' table. "Ready your ropes. Get set."

Izzy watched the jumpers lift their feet high in unison. They skipped in careful precision. Izzy concentrated on their trainers. Up and down, up and down, to the right, to the left. Izzy couldn't help being mesmerized by the footwork. It reminded him of the great boxers, the old-time fights his dad made him watch on DVD. He loved watching Muhammad Ali dance around the ring. What was it he used to say about himself? 'Float like a butterfly, sting like a bee'? The jumpers were like that: graceful but stompin'. The speed competition came next. The concentration it demanded! And when they said speed, they meant it. Izzy looked on in quiet amazement, absentmindedly tapping his feet.

But it was the freestyle competition that really sucked Izzy in. First came Gina and the Dutch Dragons. They somersaulted and even did double cartwheels in and out of the ropes. Then came the Rockin' Ropers. What was most awesome about them was that there was a guy in the group. Guys skipping? And not just to prep for boxing but in Double Dutch competitions? Izzy was intrigued.

"Joy Jumpers, ready your ropes."

The Joy Jumpers wore bright-red T-shirts and red shorts. Izzy tried not to stare too intently — he wouldn't want Mary to think he was interested! — but he couldn't help thinking they looked great.

He watched as the judges eyeballed them. He looked over at Karin. She had her fingers crossed. A whistle blew and Mary yelled: "Ready! Set! Go!" Izzy felt his heart start to beat a little harder.

Yolanda and Keisha held the ropes as Mary tumbled forward to a handstand. Shauna cartwheeled into the moving ropes to join her. They took each other's hands, and then Mary rolled over Shauna's back.

When the routine was over, Karin was squealing with delight, but Izzy couldn't help feeling like the best thing about the Joy Jumpers had been their outfits. The routine was good, but it lacked the electricity of the Dutch Dragons and the heart of the Rockin' Ropers. It was what Felix would call a boxer who didn't take any chances: it was safe.

The Joy Jumpers needed something a little extra.

But what?

The Joy Jumpers ended up taking fourth place, which at least got them to the regionals. There was no way Karin was going to leave without congratulating the older girls.

"You guys were great," she told the team.

Keisha asked Izzy what he thought. Izzy hedged. "Not bad," he said softly, trying not to make eye contact with Mary.

The Dutch Dragons walked by. "Now that's a real trophy," Yolanda said admiringly. "But we'll never see one like that."

Izzy noticed that Yolanda could be a little negative.

"What are you trying to say?" Keisha looked defensive.

"Certain people need to step it up," Yolanda replied.

Mary tried to squelch the tension. "We still qualified for the city finals," she said.

Yolanda seemed to be getting more worked up. "But we won't get past the finals with that whack routine you made up."

Whack routine? That's harsh, thought Izzy.

"I spent hours on that routine!" protested Mary.

Izzy could testify to that. He'd seen her through the window. But he didn't want to make Mary crosser, so he kept his mouth shut.

"You should be watching your feet in the ropes instead of worrying about what I'm doing," Mary told Yolanda.

"Whatever," Yolanda replied. "The routine is whack. Right, Izzy?"

Uh-oh. They were trying to drag him into it.

"Not my business," he said diplomatically. And then, because he didn't want to be questioned further, he added: "My dad's making dinner. We've got to go."

Karin looked confused. "No, we haven't."

"Yes, we have."

Izzy took one last look at the Joy Jumpers and turned away, dragging his sister and her friends with him.

CHAPTER FIVE

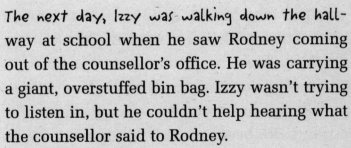

The next day, Izzy was walking down the hall-way at school when he saw Rodney coming out of the counsellor's office. He was carrying a giant, overstuffed bin bag. Izzy wasn't trying to listen in, but he couldn't help hearing what the counsellor said to Rodney.

"Don't be embarrassed. Your dad is having a hard time and people want to help."

Izzy stopped in his tracks.

"Thanks," he heard Rodney mumble. It was the most polite thing he'd ever heard the guy say.

"Now, let us know if the clothes don't fit,"

the counsellor said.

"Okay, Ms Roberts," Rodney muttered, and left the office.

Izzy pressed his back against a locker and hoped Rodney wouldn't notice him lingering there. No such luck. It was as if Rodney had sniffed him out.

"What are you looking at?" he barked.

Izzy shrugged. Rodney sneered, then dumped the bag of hand-me-downs into a school bin. Then he ran off down the hallway as if he were being chased – or maybe, in Rodney's case, it was more like he was chasing somebody.

So . . . Rodney had a secret. Maybe his life at home had something to do with his bullying behaviour. Maybe he wasn't as tough as he looked. If Izzy had been somebody else, he might have been happy to discover his opponent's secret. But Izzy was Izzy, and instead it just made him sad.

When necessary, Daniels Gym could look like a professional boxing arena. With the lights dimmed and folding chairs encircling the ring, it resembled the arenas Izzy saw in the black-and-white pictures on the gym's wall.

The exhibition match was starting in minutes, and a hush had descended upon the crowd. Izzy's plan was to tune everyone and everything out. He remained in the locker room until the last possible second, listening to his MP3 player and practising his moves.

He was working on his footwork when his dad arrived.

"You're up, Iz," he said.

Izzy took his headphones off, and stared in the mirror.

"Showtime," he told his reflection.

Izzy tried not to look into the audience as he entered the ring. If he exchanged a funny look with Lil' Earl, it might throw him. He kept his eyes straight ahead and took a seat in the corner.

His dad took him by the shoulders and stared into his eyes.

"You okay?" he asked.

"Yeah, I think so," Izzy answered.

"I know so." Izzy's dad gave him a penetrating stare. "Now show me that game face," he instructed. Izzy gave a stern, grizzled look. "That's it," said Mr Daniels. "Who's the greatest?"

"I am," Izzy replied, trying to believe it was true. He tried not to gag as his dad quickly stuffed the mouthpiece in his mouth.

"Remember." Mr Daniels's voice was solemn. "Keep your elbows low and your jabs high."

The referee's voice boomed: "In this corner, weighing in at 156 pounds, Rodney Tyler."

Until this second, Izzy had avoided looking at his opponent. Now his gaze fell on Rodney, and he all but shuddered. Could it be that Rodney had developed more muscles in the last 24 hours? His shirt and shorts were tattered and torn, as if they couldn't contain his oversized muscles. One of his boxing gloves even had a hole in it.

As Rodney glared at him, Mr Daniels gave Izzy some last bits of inspiration: "Remember, '20 per cent talent, 80 per cent heart'." Izzy took one last glance at Rodney, and hoped his father had it right. Because if it was actually '20 per cent talent, 80 per cent muscle', he was in trouble.

When his dad stepped out of the ring, Izzy jumped to his feet.

"And in this corner," announced the referee, "weighing 148 pounds, Izzy 'The Incredible' Daniels!"

Izzy danced into the centre ring to bump Rodney's gloves with his own.

"That'll be the last times your gloves touch me, chump," Rodney hissed.

Izzy and Rodney were different kinds of fighter – Izzy was speedy, while Rodney was all brute strength – but basically, they were evenly matched. The first round ended as

Rodney finally made contact with Izzy's chest, scoring a point.

"Incredible?" Rodney shouted to the crowd, motioning to Izzy. "Incredibly lame!"

Mr Daniels mopped the sweat off Izzy's brow, offering him water and advice.

"Izzy, you've got to watch his moves. He swings wild. He'll get tired. Wait him out. He's got power but no skill."

"He's fighting dirty, Dad." Izzy said. In between rounds, Rodney had taken a swipe at him without the ref seeing.

"You just stay with him and find your rhythm," Mr Daniels said encouragingly. "You got this!"

"Okay, Dad. I got it."

Round Two started and Izzy heard his dad's voice in his head: "Watch his moves. Stay with him. Find your rhythm." He ducked every one of Rodney's jabs. Around and around they went. He feared this round would end like the first one. He listened in his head for more of his dad's wisdom. He concentrated, searching for inspiration.

Suddenly, a rhythm filled his head. *Ba-bump, ba-bump, ba-bump*. The rhythm of trainers hitting the floor in brilliant precision to the whirring sound of a rope spinning fast. The sound of Double Dutch stepping filled Izzy up. All of a sudden, he started to move quicker.

He darted and ducked. He threw a jab, then an uppercut. He danced to the left and to the right. He bobbed and he weaved.

His movements were graceful and fluid, and try as he might, Rodney couldn't make contact. The more Izzy concentrated on the rhythm in his head, the more agile he became. Rodney, on the other hand, was getting more tired. He lumbered around the ring, swinging at the air, until finally, exhausted, he fell to the ground with an inglorious thump.

The crowd grew silent as the judges whispered to one another. Finally, the ref called it: "Winner: Daniels."

As the crowd cheered and Izzy raised his hands triumphantly in the air, he thought "Golden Gloves, here I come."

After the fight, Izzy headed to the locker room to pack his gym bag. Chuck and Lil' Earl tagged along; they couldn't stop talking about Izzy's big win.

"Did you see Rodney's face?" asked Chuck, smiling.

Lil' Earl joined in on the fun. "Thinks he's all that, messing with people. I would have put him on the mat with a knockout."

Just then, Felix appeared in the doorway.

"It's not about knocking someone out, Earl," he said wisely. "It's about scoring points with your combinations and footwork. It's about endurance and what's up here," he said, pointing to his head.

Izzy knew that Felix was right. There was a lot more to boxing than just punching somone out, like a bully would.

That night Izzy celebrated with his dad and Karin. As happy as he was the entire time, something was nagging at him. Felix's words had stuck in his mind, and he had to do something about it. So, when his dad and sister turned on the TV after dinner, Izzy said he had to run an errand.

He walked through the streets, finally stopping in front of a building. Was this Rodney's apartment? He took a chance, rang the bell, put down the bin bag of clothes he'd rescued from the bin at school earlier, and rushed across the street so he'd remain unseen. He watched the door open and held his breath as Rodney stared menacingly at the bag before taking it inside.

Phew.

CHAPTER SIX

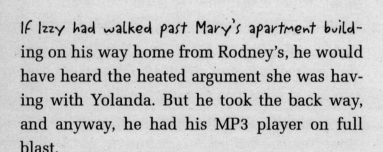

If Izzy had walked past Mary's apartment build-ing on his way home from Rodney's, he would have heard the heated argument she was hav-ing with Yolanda. But he took the back way, and anyway, he had his MP3 player on full blast.

"But we need you," Mary shouted.

"I didn't get into this to play games, Mary," Yolanda yelled back. "I'm in it to win."

Izzy entered the house, just as Yolanda stalked off, leaving Mary standing by herself.

After a snack and more praise from his dad,

Izzy went to his bedroom. Something told him he wasn't going to fall asleep quite yet, and when he glanced out of the window and saw Mary sitting alone on the fire escape, he knew his instincts were correct.

"Hey, don't jump," Izzy called out. How come he couldn't help teasing the girl? "It can't be that bad."

Mary grimaced. "Corny much?" she shot back.

Izzy laughed. Who was she calling corny? He was about to throw another zinger her way when he noticed her face had a funny puffy look to it.

"Are you crying?" he asked.

"No."

"Then why is your face all wet?"

"Why do you have so many questions?"

Sheesh, can't a guy be nice? Izzy wondered. "I'm just asking. Trying to help you out."

Mary didn't say anything for a moment. "It's nothing you can help me with," she said, sounding unusually defeated. "I heard you beat Rodney."

She crossed the fire escape to come and sit next to him. Mary smelled like toothpaste and lotion, the fancy kind of lotion that has perfume in it, like Izzy's mum used to use.

"What?" Izzy said with a smile. "Are you keeping tabs on me?"

"You wish."

Izzy told her he'd beaten Rodney and that he was going to the Golden Gloves.

"Must be nice," said Mary.

"Yeah," said Izzy, feeling a little like he was lying. "It's cool. My dad's happy."

Just then, Mary's mum called from inside the house. She wanted Mary to wash the dishes.

Izzy watched as Mary sighed noisily, then got up to go.

"What?" he teased. "You aren't gonna say good night?"

"Good night, Izzy," said Mary.

"'night," said Izzy. He suddenly felt a quickening in his chest. He didn't like it. "Hey, Mary," he called.

"What?"

"Since I'm in training, I need my sleep. Try not to snore tonight."

Mary shook her head. "Go away," she said, and went back inside.

Izzy snorted loudly. She slammed the window shut.

The next day at school, Izzy, Chuck and Lil' Earl ran into Rodney and his boys.

"I want a rematch," said Rodney.

"Just let it go," Izzy replied.

"What are you? Chicken?" Rodney said. He made some chicken sounds at Izzy then knocked Izzy's books right out of his hands.

Izzy couldn't believe his nerve. Why did Rodney always have to be such a bully?

On the way to the gym the next day, Izzy

42

walked past Mary's house. He caught Mary, Keisha and Shauna engaged in a war of words. He couldn't help but take a closer look. Keisha was talking vociferously. "I'm just saying, Tasha isn't that bad."

Mary rolled her eyes up to the streetlight.

"Girlfriend's got like two left feet. And not hers."

"What about Donzia?"

Mary looked even more irritated at Shauna's suggestion. "Double-handed," she said with a sigh.

"What about my cousin?"

"Aubrina?" Mary chortled. "She's almost blind."

Shauna corrected her. "It's called extreme myopia."

Just then, Mary noticed Izzy. She barely looked at him before she said, "Go away, Izzy. Not in the mood."

Of course, having Mary tell him to shoo made him very defensive.

"Hey. What did I do?"

"Nothing," Keisha told him. "She's just mad. Yolanda quit the team."

"Why? She finally figured out Double Dutch is lame?"

"No." Shauna sounded wistful. "She thinks we are. She joined the Dutch Dragons."

"Now we're down a jumper again," Keisha said.

"And the city finals are coming up," Mary added.

"You're kidding, right?" Izzy made a point of laughing in their faces. "Anybody can jump some rope. Shoot. My little sister's free."

Mary crossed her arms over her chest and glared at Izzy. She didn't look happy.

"If it's so easy, you do it."

Izzy loved a challenge, but this was too much!

"Come on with the come on," he said. "I got a couple of minutes to school y'all."

"Fine," huffed Mary. She turned away from

him and towards her teammates. "Keisha. Shauna." She handed them the ropes. As soon as they started to turn, Mary jumped in. She was fast. She was determined. Izzy had to admit: she was awesome.

"Go, Mary," Keisha and Shauna chanted. "Show him, girl."

Mary jumped out of the ropes. Izzy noticed that she'd barely broken a sweat. She smiled wickedly as she turned to him.

"On you, boxer boy," she said tauntingly.

So this is how she wants to play it, thought Izzy. He had to step up.

"Bring it on, jump girl," he replied. He watched as Keisha and Shauna turned the ropes. The sounds of a Brooklyn morning were all around him: the delivery trucks honking, the little kids walking to school. Out of the corner of his eye he saw Karin emerge from the brownstone. She was sitting on the stoop and watching. The ropes whirled; Izzy bobbed back and forth waiting to jump in.

"Any day," called Mary.

"I got this," Izzy shot back. He just couldn't pick the right time. The ropes were going so fast. Finally, he steeled himself, took a deep breath and jumped in. He expected to jump *with* the ropes. But he jumped into them. They jumbled around him, swinging into his face.

"Ow!" he shouted. His nose burned.

"'nough said," Mary snapped dismissively. "Now go."

Izzy hoped he didn't look as embarrassed as he felt.

"Hey, I was just kidding around," he said. "One more 'gin."

Mary relented. This time Izzy didn't watch the ropes. Instead, he closed his eyes and listened to the rhythm of the ropes as they grazed the pavement. He concentrated so hard, until he heard nothing but that sound. And then he jumped in again.

The ropes didn't hit him in the face this time. In fact, no part of Izzy's body touched a rope as he jumped. Faster and faster he went as the ropes pulsated around him. He went incredibly fast, maybe even faster than Mary.

A minute later, he jumped out. He had to get to school. He walked away, leaving four stunned jump-ropers and Karin in his wake. No one could see, but he was glowing with pride. He was happy. In fact, he was even happier than he'd been the day before when he won the exhibition fight against Rodney.

CHAPTER SEVEN

Izzy was glad to have the gym to himself. He began his training, as always, by jumping rope. He was focusing on his feet, criss-crossing his left foot over his right, as he sped up the rope. That was all he was thinking about when the girls entered the gym. They found him in the darkened corner, and waited for him to notice them.

"Hey," said Keisha.

Izzy blushed, feeling for a second like he'd been caught. It took him a second to regain his composure, to realize that he jumped rope all the time as part of his training!

"What are you guys doing here?" he asked.

"Looking for you," said Shauna.

"Found me," replied Izzy. "So?"

"You jump pretty fast."

Izzy's chest puffed out. "Well, I do have some skills," he said, not at all modestly.

"At what? Bragging?" Mary baulked.

Shauna got straight to the point. "We want you to join our team," she said.

Huh? thought Izzy. They couldn't mean what he thought they meant, could they?

"What team?" he asked, because he needed to be sure.

"The Joy Jumpers," she answered.

Izzy couldn't help it. He started to laugh. His laughter – the only laughter, since no one else joined him – resounded off the walls of the empty gym. When he stopped finally, he was greeted with silence.

"Wait. For real?" he asked.

"Yes," Keisha answered.

"*Your* jump-rope team?" Izzy baulked.

"Yeah," said Shauna.

"Okay, y'all are seriously trippin'."

This time Mary stepped in. "No, we're not. The city finals are in a couple of weeks and the competition is super-tough."

"And Izzy, you're a fast jumper. You said it yourself. You've got skills," said Keisha.

"I'm sorry for y'all," said Izzy, shaking his head sorrowfully. "But I can't go out like that. Jumping rope isn't me."

"Why?" Keisha wanted to know.

"Just isn't."

Izzy knew that wasn't enough of an answer, but he didn't have a more insightful response.

"You jump rope all the time," Shauna said.

"Yeah, for boxing, not for whatever it is y'all do."

"You scared your boys will laugh at you?" Mary looked Izzy straight in the eye when she asked that. Her gaze was piercing.

"Come on, Izzy." Shauna was practically

begging now. "We really need you."

But Izzy wouldn't budge. "No," he said.

"Forget him," Mary told her teammates finally. The girls turned to leave.

But once they had gone, the truth became clear to Izzy. He regretted what he'd just done. He thought about going after them.

Then he thought better of it.

No, he should. He started to run. He could catch up with them if he ran.

But then he glanced at the wall of black-and-white pictures. There was his dad at the Golden Gloves. And Izzy changed his mind.

That night, Izzy dreamed of doing Double Dutch. In the dream, the music was pounding and he was cartwheeling in and out of the ropes while Mary cheered for him. He woke up in a tangle of sheets. The room was totally dark. He got up and staggered, half asleep, to the window to see if she was there. But it was the dead of night and, of course, Mary was fast asleep. Izzy wondered if maybe she was dreaming about him too.

The next night, after discovering that Mr Daniels was making his infamous chilli again, Izzy went to get pizza for himself and Karin. Who should he run into at the pizza place but Keisha and Shauna? Before they could say anything, he beat them to the punch.

"The answer is still no," he said.

"We don't want you to be on the team," Keisha told him.

Izzy couldn't help feeling disappointed. They'd sure given up on him quickly.

"Good," he said, "'cause it wasn't happening."

"We just want you to fill in until we find somebody else," said Shauna.

"Fill in?" Izzy asked.

He took a deep breath. His nostrils filled with the smell of baking pizza dough.

"Yep," said Keisha. "Stand in as a fourth so

we can plan our routine right while we look for someone."

So I wouldn't actually be on the team, thought Izzy. Shauna said what he was thinking out loud.

"So, you wouldn't actually be on the team."

He could live with that.

CHAPTER EIGHT

Apparently, Mary hadn't been in on the other girls' plan, because when she found out, she went ballistic.

"Over my dead body," she told them. Izzy had been such a jerk – she didn't need to be rejected *again*. Keisha and Shauna told her to consider the alternatives, of which there were none. Mary relented, but she wasn't happy about it.

So, on the morning of what was to be his first practice as a temporary member of the Joy Jumpers, Izzy awoke to a shrill and not very kind wake-up call. It was 5:45 a.m.

"Izzy, wake up," Mary demanded from her bedroom. "It's time for practice."

Izzy found his dad and Karin in the kitchen. Mr Daniels was making yet another attempt at fixing Karin's hair.

"What's got you out of bed so early?" his dad wanted to know.

"Couldn't sleep," Izzy lied. "What are you guys doing up?"

"School pictures," his father explained.

"Ow," Karin said.

Izzy refused to work out where he'd be seen by anyone he knew. So he offered Daniels Gym as a place to meet. They'd been there for half an hour already, and so far they hadn't even started practising. Izzy didn't want to say anything, but maybe this was why they had come fourth the last time.

"Hey, if this is jump-rope practice, why aren't we jumping?" he asked.

"First, we stretch," Mary said. "Then we run, for stamina."

Izzy guffawed. "Y'all are trippin'. It's just Double Dutch."

It was like three sets of daggers were beaming into him.

"Just Double Dutch?"

"This is a sport, just like football or basketball or boxing."

Gosh, these girls just wouldn't let it go.

"A bunch of girls singing and jumping through some ropes ain't a sport."

"Then let's see you do something," Mary challenged him. "And I don't mean speed jumping."

"You mean one of those little tricks y'all do?"

"Yeah. Do a side step."

"Bring it," said Izzy. He had to admit he was enjoying the tussle. "What little song should I sing? 'Ring Around the Roses'? What?"

"We don't sing," said Mary. "We jump."

At that, Shauna and Keisha started turning the ropes.

Izzy stood apprehensively as he watched.

"What are you waiting for?" Mary taunted him.

"Nothing," said Izzy, and he jumped in.

Mary followed him. She did a karate kick then segued into a side step.

"Do it," she commanded.

Izzy tried. He hopped on one foot, but couldn't manage to extend his leg all the way without the rope hitting it. The girls laughed.

"See? Not so easy, huh?" Mary said.

Izzy tried not to sound as defensive as he felt.

"Look, y'all said you just needed someone to fill in. That's what I'm here for. I don't need to know all that. So do you want to practise or not?"

Finally, they got down to business.

Later, in the privacy of his bedroom, with the blinds closed, Izzy practised Mary's karate-kick-to-side-step move in front of the mirror.

He had to admit: it wasn't exactly easy.

"Come on, man," he told himself. "You can do this. If she can do it, you can do it."

He tried it again and still didn't get it right.

Izzy wasn't used to failure. So he kept trying. He wouldn't go to sleep that night until he got it right.

At the next practice, Mary wanted to start with speed jumping.

"I think we can take five seconds off if we try," she said.

"How 'bout freestyle?" Izzy asked.

He didn't want to sound too eager.

"We don't have that much time to watch you try to freestyle," Mary said as the rest of her teammates laughed.

"Just turn the ropes," Izzy said with characteristic swagger.

Izzy concentrated on the rhythm, then jumped in. He'd mastered the karate-kick side step. He'd also mastered the buffalo shuffle, heel touch, lunge and fling.

The girls watched, mouths agape.

"And what?" Izzy boasted.

He couldn't help but grin. It wasn't just that he'd shown the girls up – he'd really enjoyed himself.

CHAPTER NINE

People were starting to notice that something was up with Izzy. His sister Karin had spied him on more than one occasion dancing in his room. During practice, his dad kept asking him where his head was. Tammy, the only female student at the gym, had caught a glimpse of him practising with the Joy Jumpers. And who couldn't see that he was tired?

Izzy wouldn't admit it, but his new routine was running him ragged. Training at Double Dutch while going to school – and preparing for the Golden Gloves – it was getting to him.

And it showed in his game.

He was in the ring sparring with Tammy, while Mr Daniels coached from the sidelines.

"Izzy," his dad called after Tammy scored an easy point, "wake up out there."

Izzy shook his head from side to side to wake himself up. It didn't work.

Tammy ducked and weaved around the ring. He tried to follow her, but his legs felt heavy and his knees ached from all the jumping. He stood still and tried to anticipate her next move. She bobbed towards him. A quick uppercut, a jab. Before he knew it, Tammy – Tammy! – had backed Izzy into the ropes. He tried to free himself, but his legs weren't following the orders his brain was giving them. Next thing he knew, he'd fallen. So only he could hear it, Tammy whispered, "Girl boxer, one. Boy Double Dutcher, zero."

Izzy opened his eyes and blinked hard at the cement ceiling.

For the rest of the practice session, Izzy's mind was on Tammy. He tried not to let it bother him, but he couldn't help himself. It wasn't that he was upset she'd beaten him; clearly, he was off his game and he knew exactly why. But there was something about her performance in the ring that was qualitatively different from his own: she wasn't like Rodney who boxed because he liked beating people up. No, for Tammy, boxing was about way more than that. And most importantly, Tammy was having fun.

Funny, it took seeing someone else having fun to make him realize . . . he wasn't having fun. And that maybe he hadn't been having fun for a while now. Izzy could remember having fun in the ring — playing dumb games with Lil' Earl and Chuck, replaying old Mike Tyson fights punch for punch with Felix, but that had been a while ago. Now it seemed he had more fun when he jumped.

He couldn't even let himself think that.

After practice, Izzy waited for Tammy outside the locker room. Finally, she emerged.

"Hey, Tammy. Nice work."

Tammy looked sceptical. "Mmmm-hmmm," she muttered suspiciously. "What's up?"

"About that boy Double Dutching thing . . . I, uh–"

"What?" Tammy's eyes narrowed.

Izzy felt just as cornered as he had with her in the ring.

"I'm trying to keep that quiet."

"I bet you are," Tammy sniffed.

"So–" Oh, man, she was really making him work here. "Calm down," said Tammy. "I won't say anything as long as you stop all the girl-boxer jokes – especially around Chuck."

Izzy laughed. He could do that.

"You like Chuck." He said it as if it were a statement of fact rather than a question. Tammy shot him a withering look. Izzy knew

Izzy Daniels trained hard every day for the boxing championship. If he took the title, he'd be the third generation of Daniels men to win.

To get in shape for his boxing match,
Izzy ran through the streets of Brooklyn,
worked on his footwork, skipped
and sparred with other boxers at his gym.

One day during a training run, Izzy saw his
neighbour Mary playing Double Dutch with her
friends. Something about those spinning ropes
and Mary's cool moves made him stop and stare.

Mary's passion for Double Dutch was contagious. Izzy saw how much fun she had and wanted to try his hand at it.

When Izzy decided to become a member of Mary's Double Dutch team, he kept it a secret. He wasn't sure how his dad – or the other guys – would react to the news.

Izzy wanted to follow in his father's footsteps, but he just didn't have as much passion for boxing as he did for Double Dutch.

Once he started practising, Izzy couldn't get Double Dutch out of his head. Soon, Izzy had some moves of his own.

Thanks to Izzy, the Hot Chilli Steppers
reworked their routine and wowed the
crowd at the Double Dutch city finals.

he couldn't push it.

"Cool," he said. "I can do that."

Izzy was slouching on the sofa, worn out from the day, when his dad appeared before him. He had a gigantic smile on his face.

"Got something to cheer you up," he boomed. He held up a DVD. *Knockouts, Volume 4.*

Somehow, Karin had already learned of Izzy's loss. (Was she always spying on him or what?) She didn't miss the opportunity to tease him. "Of course, they weren't knocked out by a girl," she mocked.

Mr Daniels looked sternly at his daughter, then returned his attention to Izzy. He forced a smile. "Every great boxer learns from their mistakes," he said.

"Great," Izzy said sarcastically. He yawned.

"We can watch it until the chilli is ready," Mr Daniels said.

Now it was Karin's turn to be sarcastic.

"Great," she muttered.

CHAPTER TEN

Izzy was a perfectionist. Even though he didn't want to be a permanent member of the Joy Jumpers, and even though he was really a boxer – a boxer who was going to *win* the Golden Gloves – he couldn't help feeling that, in the words of Yolanda, the Joy Jumpers's routines were whack.

And because he was a perfectionist, and because he was the son of a Golden Gloves champ, who'd drummed it into his head to always do the best he could, Izzy had a hard time living with the fact that the routines were whack.

In short: he couldn't help himself. He had to do something about it.

"Come on Izzy, let's work the freestyle," said Mary at the beginning of practice.

Izzy hesitated for a moment, then realized he should just come right out and say it. He knew he needed to be kind but firm. So he looked Mary in the eyes and said, "Listen, I think we need a new routine."

Mary looked surprised. "Why?"

As much as Izzy liked teasing Mary, he didn't want to outright hurt her.

"Because yours is, you know . . ."

"What?"

Clearly the girl didn't get it. It looked as if he was going to have to be honest – brutally so.

"Boring," he said.

Mary was immediately defensive.

"What do you know?" she snarled.

Her face contorted into a belligerent frown. Izzy had to admit: even when she was pouting like a little girl, Mary looked cute.

"I know the judges at regionals weren't feeling you," he argued.

Mary had to admit he had a point there.

Izzy didn't know what to say next. He didn't exactly know what was wrong with the girls' routine, only that it lacked something. For some reason, he thought back to his match with Tammy the other day. She was so playful in the ring, the same way he'd been before boxing had become about competition. And then, at the same time as he realized what was wrong with his boxing game . . . he knew what was wrong with the Joy Jumpers' routine: it wasn't fun.

He'd come to a giant realization. Meanwhile, Mary and the girls were still staring at him, awaiting an explanation.

"It's the difference between Double Dutching for competition and doing it for fun," explained Izzy, who was now recalling some kids he'd seen Double Dutching on the street the other day. He'd been on a jog, and he couldn't help noticing how happy they'd looked. Their routines weren't perfect. Actually, they didn't even have routines! But their carefree attitudes were flawless.

"So what do we do, Mr Smarty?"

Mary's hands were on her hips now.

He'd have to show it to her, so she could see for herself. "Well, I do have one idea."

And so the Joy Jumpers — led by their stand-in, Izzy — went on a field trip. Luckily for Izzy, the kids he'd seen on the street were there again. Hip-hop blared from a boom box. Izzy, Mary, Keisha and Shauna took seats on a stoop, watching.

The routines they did weren't precise — they weren't even routines, really. They did springs, they leaped, they cartwheeled and they danced. The Joy Jumpers did all that, only there was no joy in their jumping, no spark. These kids were smokin', and they were having fun, too.

"They're good," Mary said finally. "Who are

they? And are they competing? I thought I knew every team out there."

"Maybe they are just jumping to jump," said Izzy. Like I used to box to box, he thought. It's not all about the competition.

On the way home, the girls were pumped. So was Izzy.

"That was so amazing," said Mary.

"Hey!" Keisha hooted. "Check this out."

She stopped in the middle of the pavement and freestyled.

"Y'all feel me?" she cried.

Shauna spun around herself. "I feel you!" she yelled.

Mary couldn't let them have all the fun. She did a few moves, then started to chant — like she used to when she was a kid playing jump-rope games in the playground.

"My name is Mary!"

"Yeah, Mary!" Keisha and Shauna sang back.

"I'm rough and tough."

"Yeah."

"You get in my way—"

"Yeah."

"I'll mess you up."

"Oooh, she thinks she's bad!" Keisha howled.

"I know I'm bad," chanted Mary.

"Ooh, she thinks she's cool," Shauna chanted.

"Cool enough to steal your moves," sang Mary. She had a huge grin on her face. She turned to Izzy. "You go."

Izzy was revved up, too. He did a front handspring, then chanted, "My name is Izzy."

"Yeah," called the girls.

"I'm smooth and I'm clean. When I jump rope . . . all the girls scream."

"Ooh, he thinks he's good," Keisha sang.

"I rule this hood."

"Ooh, he makes me holler," Mary hooted.

"Watch me while I pop my collar," Izzy rhymed.

They were laughing at the top of their

lungs, when a familiar — and not friendly — voice interrupted.

"Hey. Look at daddy's boy."

Izzy stopped freestyling.

"Rodney," he said somberly.

"Well wasn't that just adorable?" Rodney squealed in a high-pitched voice. "Maybe I should show these girls what a loser you really are."

"Loser?" Izzy shook his head. This guy was unbelievable. "Last time I checked, I won that match."

Rodney started walking towards Izzy, trying to be as intimidating as possible.

"You don't want to do this," said Izzy.

Rodney got closer. They were standing face to face, at which point Mary ran to the ice stand, grabbed a jug of ice and poured it over Rodney's head.

"Hey, Rodney," she said. "Why don't you chill?" She turned to Izzy and grabbed his elbow. "Come on," she said, then pulled him down the street. They started to run.

Of course, Rodney wouldn't have been Rodney if he didn't chase after them.

Around a corner, down an alley, Izzy could hear the sound emanating from Rodney's gigantic trainers clump-clumping after them. At first, they were loud, but then as the Joy Jumpers gained speed, the sounds coming from Rodney grew more distant, and Izzy gained confidence. He leaped over a bag of rubbish and turned it into a handspring.

"Show-off," said Mary with a laugh.

Excited by what they'd seen and pumped up with energy, the Joy Jumpers sped off, losing Rodney for good. Or at least for now.

CHAPTER ELEVEN

Izzy and Mary walked home together through the neighbourhood. The pavement glittered; the outdoor cafés were hopping with well-dressed men and women back from the office. Kids and parents lined up outside the ice stand that served funny flavours like Orange Blossom Cream and Vanilla Ambrosia. It was one of those perfect nights. Izzy said goodbye by doing a shuffle-half-step tog, looking entirely silly. Then he headed home and crept upstairs to bed. A few minutes later, he heard Mary's voice through his open window.

"Hey, goofy," said Mary. "Thanks."

"For what?" Izzy asked. He crawled through his window and climbed towards Mary's fire escape.

Mary shrugged. "Nothing," she said. "Everything," she added. "I don't know."

"Man, those jumpers were cool, huh?" said Izzy, thinking back on the day.

"Well, well . . ." Mary's voice was kind but teasing. "Look who likes Double Dutch."

"Who?" asked Izzy. Izzy thought for a second, then admitted the truth. "I don't know. I guess I do. It's just something about it."

Mary seemed to know what he was thinking.

"Better than boxing?" she asked. "It's okay if you do, you know."

"It's complicated," Izzy said with a sigh. "I mean, my dad . . . boxing is kind of his thing."

Mary seemed to know just what he was talking about.

"That's what I thought about ballet," she

said. "Every September, my mum would sign me up. It was like school started, so ballet started. I thought she loved it. But last year I finally said, 'Mum, I hate ballet'. And you know what she said? 'Good, because you look like a horse galloping across the stage anyway'."

She really *did* get it. Izzy laughed – both because it was funny to imagine a little version of Mary looking like a horse, and because knowing someone else understood the pressure that he was feeling was a nice relief.

Izzy got serious again.

"But boxing is all my dad has," he said mournfully.

"No," said Mary kindly. "He has you."

Izzy smiled. "Corny much?" he said.

"I'm just saying," said Mary with a shrug.

Izzy thanked her. "It's just not that easy," he explained.

Evening had given way to night, and Mary and Izzy had said all there was to say. It was time to call it a night. Izzy knew he had to do something to cap off their evening, to show Mary how special it had been for him, but she beat him to it when she leaned in and kissed him. It was a quick kiss, but it left Izzy awash in the smell of her perfumey lotion and her coconut shampoo.

"So I guess I'll go work on that new routine," Mary said. "See you tomorrow?"

"Bright and early," said Izzy, who couldn't wait for tomorrow to begin.

Izzy tried to be as quiet as possible as he made his way back inside. He was smiling, the memory of Mary's kiss – who knew lips could be so soft? – still fresh in his mind.

His feet had just hit the floor of his bedroom when the lights turned on.

"Where have you been?" asked Mr Daniels in a gravelly voice.

Izzy could hear the TV in the background. From the sound of it, his dad had fallen asleep to the news.

Izzy turned to face his dad. Mr Daniels had a dour expression; he was clearly not happy.

"I was . . . uh . . . out . . . with my friends."

"I see," said Izzy's dad. "So I guess you were busy."

Izzy couldn't see where his dad was going with this.

"A little," he answered.

"Too busy to remember you had a practice match?" his dad asked. "Or that your curfew was two hours ago?"

Practice match!? So that's what this was about? Curfew! He couldn't imagine his dad really cared about that.

Izzy's dad looked stern. "What's been going on with you lately?"

Everything, Izzy thought.

"Nothing," he said.

"Something's going on," said Mr Daniels. "I want us to sit down and talk about it. Are you nervous about the match?"

Could his dad be more off base?

"No, Dad," Izzy replied.

"Don't lose focus now," said his dad. His tone had turned encouraging.

"I'm not, Dad," Izzy said in his most insistent voice.

Mr Daniels looked concerned. "Izzy, I just don't want you to disappoint yourself in the ring."

Izzy thought for a moment. "I won't be late again," he said.

CHAPTER TWELVE

Izzy was standing in front of his locker, trying to work out how he could explain to his maths teacher why he kept dozing off during today's quiz, when a giant weight slammed against him. Notebooks and textbooks tumbled out of his locker as Izzy struggled to regain his balance. He'd just managed to do so when he got slammed again. This time, he turned to see his attacker: it was Rodney, with his buddy Devon.

"Yeah," Devon said.

Rodney's face was red with fury. "Where you gonna run to now, fool?"

"Yeah," Devon said. Did this guy have any other words in his vocabulary?

The two thugs were closing in on him, when Izzy noticed Ms Roberts, the counsellor, walking down the hall towards them. He smiled mischievously, then spoke in his loudest voice.

"Look, man—" Izzy actually tried to sound weak and pathetic as he whined, "—don't hit me. I'll give you my lunch money."

Poor, befuddled Rodney didn't know what the heck Izzy was going on about.

"What?" he barked angrily.

Meanwhile, Ms Roberts made a beeline for the boys.

"Mr Tyler! Mr James!" she shouted.

Rodney swallowed hard.

"Ms Roberts," he stammered.

Ms Roberts shot him an unforgiving glare.

"Come with me," she ordered.

"Detention?" Now Rodney really did sound pathetic.

Ms Roberts nodded. "And it's free, so you won't need Mr Daniels's lunch money."

She ushered Rodney and Devon down the hall. Rodney looked back. The evil glint in his eyes told Izzy this was far from being over.

It didn't take long for the Joy Jumpers to implement the changes in their freestyle routine, and soon, inspired by the group they'd seen on the street jumping rope, they were doing hand claps, one-foot tricks, dance kicks, leap-frogs, and double twists. But the big change to the routine was that their moves were no longer mechanical. They were full of life, love for the sport of Double Dutch, and fun.

The Joy Jumpers had just spent an entire practice on freestyling and were hanging out in the gym.

"That was awesome," said Keisha.

Shauna agreed. "We are going to smoke the city finals now."

Mary brought the girls back to earth.

"Sorry to rain on the Double Dutch parade, but don't we still need a fourth person for that?"

It was as if she'd just let the air out of a balloon. There was silence.

"Mary's right," said Shauna. "We've still got to find somebody."

"I just wish," stammered Keisha, then thought better of what she was going to say. "Never mind."

Mary had a suggestion. "Maybe we could beg Yolanda to come back. I mean, our routine is really tight now."

"Right," said Keisha sarcastically. "Like that's going to happen."

The mood was despondent now.

"Great," said Shauna, "we're the bomb and nobody is going to see it."

Until this moment, Izzy had watched the scene unfold as if he were an innocent bystander just there to observe. But as he listened to the girls and watched as their moods darkened, he couldn't help feeling something. Rather, he couldn't help feeling a million things.

"Maybe I can help," he said.

"You know someone?" Mary asked.

Shauna looked excited. "Yeah, who is it, Izzy?"

"Me," he said.

Mary broke the stunned silence. "What?"

Izzy grinned, and adopted his typical swagger when he said, "Well, it's obvious you're not going to find anyone as good as me, so . . ."

The next thing he knew he was enveloped in a giant Double Dutch hug. The girls were a little gross and sweaty – so was he for that matter – but none of them cared.

Shauna could barely contain herself. "We are so gonna win now."

Mary turned to Izzy. "So, superstar, what changed your mind?"

"I guess I hate to disappoint the ladies," Izzy said with a laugh.

"Oh, please!" Keisha whooped.

"What about your boys?" Mary wanted to know. Izzy felt a mild twinge of guilt when he told her he figured Chuck and Lil' Earl didn't have to know.

"Then welcome to the team," said Shauna.

Once the reality of the situation had sunk in, Izzy realized he couldn't join the Joy Jumpers – at least not if they were called the Joy Jumpers. He broke it to the group.

"I do have one condition," he said.

Mary looked at him warily. "Like what?"

"The name," said Izzy. "Come on, 'Joy Jumpers'? I can't go out like that."

Mary got all defensive, of course. Immediately, she began to resist. "I like our–"

Keisha set her straight. "We're cool with changing the name," she said. Mary shot her a look; Keisha ignored it.

Izzy rattled a few potential names off: the Brooklyn Breakers, Jump Masters . . . neither got a reaction from the girls.

"The Hot Chilli Steppers?" he asked.

The girls nodded, exchanging looks. "I love it," said Keisha. Shauna said she did, too.

"It's all right, I guess," Mary relented.

That was consensus enough for Izzy.

"Cool," he said, "Hot Chilli Steppers on three."

Izzy extended his hand; the girls followed. They counted: one, two, three, then screamed, "Hot Chilli Steppers!"

"So now that we've got a team, maybe we can enter this," said Keisha, reaching into her back pocket and pulling out a flyer for the Double Dutch Showcase, an exhibition in Harlem.

"It's in three days," said Mary.

"I don't think we're ready," said Shauna.

Izzy disagreed. "We're ready," he said.

This time Mary didn't jump to disagree with him.

"He's right, we're ready," she said.

CHAPTER THIRTEEN

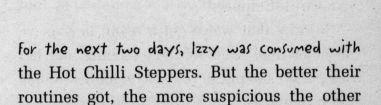

For the next two days, Izzy was consumed with the Hot Chilli Steppers. But the better their routines got, the more suspicious the other people in Izzy's life became that something strange was going on.

It was late afternoon in the Daniels house, the day of the Double Dutch Showcase, and Karin was being nosy as always. Izzy was on his way out.

"Where are you going?" Karin wanted to know.

"Nunya," Izzy mumbled in response.

"Mmmm-hmmm," Karin mumbled back.

She sounded suspicious. Mr Daniels appeared.

"Izzy's leaving," Karin said.

"Where are you going?" Mr Daniels asked.

How to lie . . . but not really lie? he thought.

"Out," Izzy answered. "With Mary."

It was the truth! Basically.

"Ooohhh!" Karin practically jumped up and down in girlish glee. She started to sing.

"Izzy and Mary, sittin' in a tree."

Sheesh! "Chill, Karin!" Izzy commanded.

Izzy's dad took a different approach than Karin. He got sensitive.

"You sure have been spending a lot of time with Mary," he remarked.

Izzy played dumb. "What?" he baulked.

"Hey," said Mr Daniels with a smile, "she's a pretty girl."

Izzy knew he hadn't told the whole truth, but he felt embarrassed – as if he had. "Dad. So can I go?"

"You could," Mr Daniels replied. "Or you could hang out with your dad."

He'd been hiding something. He held two tickets in the air and waved them joyfully.

"The Arena," he announced. "Evans/Chaves. Today."

Evans. Chaves. Oh, please say this wasn't happening!

"Today?" Izzy asked. He gulped.

"That's right," said Mr Daniels, thinking Izzy was as pleased as he was. "Me and you. We're going to see a real champ."

The look in his dad's eyes . . . Izzy just couldn't let him down. He called Mary, but got her mum instead. Mary had already left for the Double Dutch Showcase. It was too late to tell her he wouldn't be able to make it.

What do you do when what you want to do will disappoint someone you love? Izzy had been forced to make a choice. He just hoped it was the right one.

Sitting there at the fight, Izzy could just

picture Mary and the other girls waiting for him to show up. He knew they'd be disappointed – even angry – that he'd let them down.

That night, after the fight, Izzy went to his and Mary's usual spot out on the fire escape. He'd spent the entire fight not enjoying himself at all. How could he when he was consumed with guilt, not to mention the desire to be somewhere else? He didn't know what he'd say to Mary, but he had to say something.

Her window was closed; her room was dark, but something told him she was home. He called out to her.

"Pssst, Mary."

Nothing.

He got a little louder. "Mary. Open the window. Please."

Nothing.

Then, finally, he thought he saw a shadowy figure behind the curtain. Please come out, please, please come out, he thought. Finally, his prayers were answered: Mary pulled back the curtains and opened the window. She looked far from pleased.

"What?!" she barked.

Izzy knew she wouldn't be happy, but her anger caught him off guard.

"Sorry about tonight. My dad—"

Mary interrupted him. "I don't care, Izzy," she said matter-of-factly.

But Izzy had to explain. "My dad got tickets to a boxing match."

Mary stared at him, her mouth hanging open in disbelief. He couldn't believe it. Everything he said was just making things worse!

"A boxing match?" She said the words slowly and methodically. "Oh, then my bad."

"I tried to call."

"What was that going to do? You asked to be on the team, and then you just left us hanging. You had us all fooled thinking you liked Double Dutch. We looked like fools up there.

We were counting on you. But I guess this is all a joke to you."

Wow, thought Izzy, she really doesn't get it.

"What was I supposed to do?" Izzy asked.

"Make a choice," Mary said.

Izzy had made a choice, but apparently it was not the right one.

"I couldn't," he said.

"Then I'll do it for you," Mary said. "You are off the team."

"What?" Izzy couldn't believe his ears. The entire boxing match he'd been thinking about Double Dutch, replaying the routines in his head. And then this was what happened? Mary could really be punishing.

"Double Dutching is serious to us," she told him. "To me. And you showed me that I can't rely on you."

"But, Mary–" Izzy spluttered.

"Bye, Izzy," Mary said.

She closed the window, leaving him on the other side, alone and in shock.

CHAPTER FOURTEEN

Izzy returned to his old life. Or tried to. Because he'd kept his new passion a secret from everyone except the Hot Chilli Steppers themselves, returning to his old life should have been easy. But it wasn't. Izzy didn't feel the same. As much as he tried to pretend that his foray into Double Dutch had never happened, he couldn't put it out of his mind: he was always thinking about the routines; the music played in his head on an endless loop; and every night, he looked for a light in Mary's room. But it was always dark.

Spending time with his boys helped ease

the pain. He, Chuck and Lil' Earl were hanging out at the gym, watching Tammy hit the mitts. Even without a human sparring partner, Tammy couldn't help dancing around and having a good time. She slugged away.

"Lucky punch," commented Lil' Earl.

Izzy had not forgotten his conversation with Tammy and the promises they'd made to each other.

"She's not lucky," he protested. "She's good."

Lil' Earl couldn't believe his ears.

"Say what?" he said.

"Tammy's a good boxer."

Lil' Earl had to qualify that statement. "For a girl," he said with a laugh.

Izzy looked at his friend and wondered if his thinking could really be that backward. Clearly, Izzy was going to have to do some schooling.

"For anybody," Izzy told Lil' Earl. He wasn't playing now. He had to pull out the big guns.

"I remember she knocked you out last week."

Lil' Earl looked annoyed. "I told you I thought I saw a quarter on the mat," he argued.

But Izzy wasn't accepting Lil' Earl's excuses.

"Just because she's a girl, doesn't mean she can't box. Just like guys can do other stuff, too."

Izzy had had enough. As he was walking off, he heard Lil' Earl complain to Chuck.

"What's his problem?" he asked.

Izzy couldn't help but smile when he heard Chuck respond, "I think she's good, too."

The next day, Izzy's life went from bad to worse. It wasn't only his family who'd noticed that Izzy was spending a lot of time with Mary. There was someone else, too.

That someone else was Rodney, who, one recent early morning back when Izzy was a Hot Chilli Stepper, had paid a visit to the gym and got an eyeful of Izzy Double Dutching with the girls.

Now he knew Izzy's secret.

Because Rodney wasn't the brightest bulb, and because he wanted to do something that was absolutely as mean as possible, it had taken him a few days to figure out how to use Izzy's secret against him.

It was the morning, and as always, Izzy was late for his first class. He was running down the hallway when it dawned on him that something was different about the school today. There were pieces of paper taped to every surface area. Was today student elections? Had Izzy been so out of it that he'd missed that?

He stopped short to see what all the flyers were for, when he heard the sound of laughter all around him. What was everyone laughing at? He glanced at a flyer. It was pink with a picture of: *Izzy jumping Double Dutch!* Across it, written in capital letters, was the word LOSER. The people who were laughing were laughing at him.

Izzy stood flabbergasted, in horror, not knowing what to do next. He didn't even realize that Lil' Earl and Chuck had approached.

"Yo, Iz? What's up with this?" Lil' Earl was holding a flyer in the air.

"Nice legs, Isadore," said Chuck with a laugh.

"What are you trying to say?" Izzy couldn't believe this was happening.

"We're trying to say you look real pretty." Lil' Earl batted his eyelashes seductively at Izzy.

Izzy didn't get the joke. In fact, he didn't think his friends were being funny at all. He stepped up to Lil' Earl, and stood menacingly over him. Izzy could be scary sometimes – he was a teen boxing champ, after all.

Lil' Earl looked stunned.

"Yo, Iz," said Chuck. "Chill. We're just playing."

Izzy stepped back, but he was still angry.

Just then, Rodney and his bunch of thugs appeared.

"Now I see why you won't give me a rematch," Rodney said. "Too busy jumping Double Dutch." He held up the flyer. "I went with pink. Nice touch, don't you think?"

There was a ripping sound from across the hall. Izzy turned to see Mary prying flyers off of the lockers. Mary! The girl who wouldn't even talk to him! Was she sticking up for him now – or was she making fun of him also?

Izzy's head was a jumbled mess. He didn't know what to think, so instead he just ran off.

CHAPTER FIFTEEN

Mary knew she'd been too harsh on Izzy. Now it was her turn to beg forgiveness. Izzy heard the pencil ricochet off his windowpane. He heard Mary call his name. But he didn't respond. It wasn't just her. He didn't want to talk to anybody.

Izzy opened his rucksack and took out the pink flyer. He'd crumpled it up in rage. Now he uncrumpled it, smoothing out the wrinkles with the back of his hand. He sat for several seconds studying the picture. Rodney intended for Izzy to be mortified by the flyer, but in the privacy of his own room, it was having the opposite effect on Izzy. He looked at the picture and felt proud. He saw somebody who was happy. He saw someone who had skills.

Izzy kept a framed picture of his family on his bedside table. The picture had been taken before Karin was born, so it was just Izzy and his parents. In the picture, a scrawny, shrimpy Izzy was proudly sporting his Dad's old boxing gloves.

Izzy looked from the flyer to the picture, then back to the flyer. He didn't know whether to feel sad, frustrated or both. He wished life was as easy as it had been when he was five, when his mum was alive and when he thought boxing was the be-all and end-all. That was before he knew other options even existed.

Izzy crumpled the paper in an angry ball, then tossed it onto the floor. Then he turned off the lights and stared into the blackness.

If only he'd taken the time to throw the flyer

in the bin, because the next day – while tidy-ing Izzy's room – his dad found it.

Izzy's life would never be the same again.

Izzy was making a bowl of cereal for himself, when his dad said he needed to have a word with him.

"You were snooping in my rubbish?" said Izzy when he learned that his dad had seen the flyer.

"My house. My rubbish," said his father. "Now, what's this about Double Dutch?"

"Nothing," Izzy lied. It was morning, he was bleary-eyed, and he wasn't prepared for this talk.

Karin butted in. "He's just mad because some kids have been laughing at him because he's on a Double Dutch team," Karin said.

Izzy stared at his little sister in disbelief.

"Hey, I'm eight. I know things," she said with a shrug.

Mr Daniels asked what she was talking

about. Karin took it upon herself to explain.

"He's a part of the Hot Chilli Steppers. It's Mary's Double Dutch team, and Rodney found out and—"

Izzy couldn't stand this. "Shut up, Karin," he said.

"Shut don't go up, prices do, take your advice and shut up, too," Karin smart-mouthed back.

"Both of you, quiet," Mr Daniels boomed. He turned away from Izzy and towards Karin. "Go to your room," he said.

Karin left, but she wasn't happy about it. Izzy and his dad were alone.

"Is this the reason your mind has not been in the ring?" Izzy's father asked him.

Izzy was quiet. He had no lies left in him.

"Talk to me, Izzy," his dad coaxed. "Why didn't you tell me about this?"

"Because." It was all Izzy could come up with. He felt like a little kid who'd just been caught with his hand in the cookie jar – there was no real excuse for what he'd done.

"You want to elaborate on that?" Mr Daniels asked. He wasn't furious, but his tone was definitely serious.

"Because you wouldn't have heard me unless I was talking about boxing . . ." The words started coming, and so did the tears. But Izzy fought past them. "It's all you talk about," he told his dad. "It's all we talk about since mum died. And I don't even like it any more."

As he said the words, Izzy knew they were true – painfully true.

"I'm just doing it for you, and it's not fair. Just 'cause you don't have a life any more doesn't mean you have to take mine away."

As relieved as Izzy felt to finally get the words out, he was horrified to have actually said them. His dad had a miserable, pained look in his eyes.

"I'm sorry, Dad," he said.

"That's okay, Izzy," his dad replied.

Though, clearly, nothing was okay.

CHAPTER SIXTEEN

Izzy took out his frustration on the punchbag. An uppercut, a jab. He tried to channel Tammy's spirit as he bobbed and weaved. All he managed to channel was anger.

A familiar soft voice filled his ears.

"Izzy, I've been looking for you," Mary said.

Still, he kept punching.

"You found me," said Izzy as he delivered a straight jab to the bottom of the bag.

"What are you doing?" Mary asked. "Look, the girls and I were talking. I just wanted to ask you—"

Izzy interrupted her. "I'm not doing it," he said.

"What?"

"I need to focus on boxing," Izzy told her as he focused on the bag.

"I don't understand," Mary said.

"I'm a boxer," Izzy told her. "And I can't be a champion if I'm jumping rope with a bunch of girls."

If Izzy had turned to look at Mary, he would have seen that she was aghast.

"What are you talking about? Is this because of Rodney and them?"

"No," said Izzy, thinking of the sad look in his dad's eyes, "I mean . . . it's not *just* Rodney."

"You love Double Dutch, Izzy. You know you do. And you're good."

Izzy knew it was true. But still.

"I'm not doing it," he said. "I'm sorry."

"No, Izzy," Mary said. "I'm sorry."

Tammy was the next person to try to talk some sense into Izzy.

"Wassup?" she said.

Izzy was still punching away at the bag. Tammy wasn't deterred.

"Double Dutch competition's tomorrow, right?"

Izzy laid into the bag with a roundhouse.

"So that's it? You're just going to punk out because people are laughing?"

Izzy didn't have a response. Tammy kept talking.

"Look, you normally get on my nerves, but I can't let you go out like this. Imagine if I listened to every stupid comment you and your boys have made about me; I wouldn't be the best girl boxer in the city. So people make fun. I figure—" Tammy punched the bag hard enough for Izzy to feel it through the other side . . . wow, the girl really did pack a wallop, "—that's their problem."

Izzy knew that she was right. Still he couldn't do what she suggested. He wasn't sure why. Maybe he was too loyal to his dad, or maybe he was weak. Or maybe he needed one more person to show him the way.

That person ended up being the most unlike-ly person of all. It was night-time – Izzy had done a full day at the gym; in fact, he was clos-ing it down – when Rodney appeared as if out of nowhere.

"Wassup, daddy's boy?" he said. He had his thugs with him. Izzy wondered if he was in for it. "Where you running off to now? Ballet class?"

Izzy tried to ignore them.

"So what? You out of words?" taunted Rodney.

"Here's one," Izzy said. "Move."

It wasn't his cleverest retort, but he meant it.

"No," responded Rodney. "It's time for that rematch, punk. Gear up. Or are you chicken?" At that Rodney made a couple of chicken sounds. "Bawk, bawk."

Izzy decided that he might as well get it over with.

"Let's do this," he said.

Rodney's thugs formed a noisy circle around the ring. Izzy and Rodney, both in full boxing gear now, faced off.

"You're about to get schooled," said Rodney.

"Those who can't . . . teach," Izzy shot back. "Right?"

The two circled each other. Rodney threw a right punch. Izzy sidestepped it. Rodney lunged. Izzy cross-stepped around him.

"You gonna box or dance, jump-rope boy?"

"Why?" asked Izzy. "It won't change the fact that I already beat you."

"Beat you bad!" called a voice from the audience. Izzy turned to see that Chuck and Lil' Earl, having heard that something was going on at the gym, had arrived and pushed their way up to the front row. Izzy noticed that Felix was in the crowd, too.

"Watch it, man," Rodney growled.

"You think if you beat me now, it's gonna change the fact that your daddy's out of work?"

Izzy taunted.

"I'm warning you!!" Rodney yelled.

"Or that everyone just thinks of you as a loud-mouth bully?"

"Tell him, Izzy," screamed Lil' Earl.

"I said, 'watch it'," Rodney reminded him.

"You can't use fighting to get respect," Izzy told him.

Rodney rushed him. Izzy sidestepped away.

"Are you running from me, daddy's boy? Why don't you run back to your jump rope?"

"I don't need ropes to do this." Izzy did a half-shuffle tog into a box step, then met Rodney's advance by leapfrogging over him. "But with ropes, it's more impressive."

Rodney lumbered towards him, angrier and more threatening than ever.

"You know what else looks better in the ropes?" Izzy hit the mat in a push-up position and then slid through Rodney's legs. The crowd roared.

"He learned all that Double Dutching," Chuck told the stranger standing next to him.

"Yeah!" Lil' Earl clamoured. "And he's my best friend."

Rodney was beginning to feel the weight of humiliation. Izzy saw the sadness in the bully's eyes. A strange urge overcame him. He wanted to make Rodney feel better. He could let Rodney hit him – he considered that for a second. But then he thought better of it. For Rodney, boxing was about beating people up. But that's not what boxing was *really* about. Izzy knew that in his heart.

"It's over, man," Izzy said. "Let's stop this. I'm sorry about your dad. I'm sorry I beat you. I'm sorry that you're so angry, but I'm not doing this with you, man."

"Keep your sorry," Rodney groaned.

Izzy was trying to reason with the dude.

"Man, we both got a lot to be mad about. But fighting isn't going to make it better. There are more important things."

Rodney didn't want to hear it. He put up his gloves, and started towards Izzy. Izzy spun around. It threw Rodney off balance. He stumbled.

"Finish him, Izzy!" Chuck yelled from the crowd.

Izzy stood over Rodney.

"Go ahead, man," Rodney said.

But it was too easy.

"No," Izzy said. "I'm done with you. I'm done with this. I don't know about you, but I'm tired of being mad."

Izzy held out his hand to Rodney and helped him up.

When it was all over, and Felix was escorting Rodney out of the ring, Izzy heard the old man whisper, "Atta boy."

CHAPTER SEVENTEEN

The reporter stood in the centre of the auditorium.

"We're here at the Double Dutch city finals. The top three teams with the highest cumulative scores in speed, compulsory and freestyle will qualify to go to the state championship. And the winner of state could go on to compete in the world championship. This is all very exciting."

Exciting might not have been what Mary called the scene; she, Keisha and Shauna were pacing back and forth. How would the Hot Chilli Steppers do without Izzy? They'd proved at the Double Dutch Showcase that without Izzy . . . they weren't, well, much.

They had a replacement for Izzy: Shauna's extremely myopic cousin, Aubrina, a well-meaning but slightly sluggish girl.

"He's really not coming?" Keisha asked.

"I said 'no'," said Mary for what must have been the millionth time.

"But we need him," Shauna was practically whimpering.

"Why? We've got Aubrina."

Just as Mary said her name, Aubrina tripped over a gym bag.

"Izzy," said Keisha.

What was wrong with her friend? She couldn't get the drift that Izzy wasn't showing.

"Forget Izzy," Mary said, trying not to sound too frustrated. "He's not coming, okay."

"Yeah, girl," Shauna agreed. "Let it go."

But Keisha saw something they didn't. She spoke slowly and purposely.

"No. Izzy. He's here. He's here."

Shauna and Mary turned towards the auditorium's entrance. There, strutting in, carrying his gym bag, was . . .

"Izzy?" Mary called.

Izzy could have said, "Hello." Instead, he said: "You guys weren't trying to do this without me, were you?"

"We thought you quit," said Keisha.

"I did. And I'm sorry."

Mary looked annoyed.

"I'm sorry. I'm sorry. That's all you got?"

Did Mary think it was too little too late? Izzy knew he was taking a chance by coming here. As much as he adored Mary, he had to admit she could be unforgiving.

"Um, well . . ." Izzy stammered.

But Mary was just playing him.

"'Cause around here you need two 'I'm sorry's and a uniform," she cried, throwing him a Hot Chilli Stepper T-shirt. Izzy caught it and blushed.

"Izzy, what made you change your mind?"

Shauna asked.

Izzy stared intently at Mary and said, "Let's just say that sometimes you have to listen to your heart."

She stared just as intently back.

Goodbye, Aubrina, hello Izzy.

The MC used a giant megaphone to call for the teams.

"Hot Chilli Steppers! Dutch Dragons! Sunshine Steppers!"

This was the moment Izzy had been waiting for: his first official Double Dutch competition. As he ran out to face the judges, he pumped himself up: I'm slammin', I'm quick, I'm slammin', I'm quick.

"Ready your ropes," the MC demanded.

Shauna and Mary grabbed the ropes, and at the sound of the whistle, Izzy jumped in.

"Fast and furious, Iz," Shauna coached.

"You can do it," Mary told him. Hearing her say that, he knew he could.

Izzy's feet were a blur of movement. In the same way that he'd channelled Double Dutchers when he boxed, now he looked to boxing for inspiration. He moved his feet the way Felix had taught him. Up, up, up . . . 151 steps . . . 155 steps . . . 205 steps. It felt good to find strength from his boxing past.

"Dig in," Mary called out.

Izzy's performance was rewarded with . . . second place. The team was stoked.

"Ooohhh, we bad," sang Shauna as the team celebrated with a hug.

"And first place," announced the MC, "with 378 steps . . . the Dutch Dragons."

The team watched as Yolanda walked by, smirking ruefully.

"Second place. That's cute," she snipped.

The Hot Chilli Steppers refused to let it ruin their mood.

The compulsories were next. This time, Shauna and Izzy turned the ropes as Mary and Keisha performed criss-cross jumps, turns and high steps with accurate precision. Izzy concentrated on the whirling of the ropes, and didn't notice when his friends Chuck and Lil' Earl took their seats in the audience. He also didn't notice when his enemy, Rodney, arrived.

The MC coughed twice before making the announcement.

"In compulsory . . . Third place: the Sunshine Steppers. Second place: the Dutch Dragons. And first place: the Hot Chilli Steppers."

First, first! Izzy threw up his fists in triumph. He couldn't believe how happy he was. Boxing was all about winning on your own. Now he was happy because Mary and Keisha had won – he hadn't even been jumping! He couldn't help but flash Yolanda a winning grin.

"This is my favourite part of the competition," the MC announced. "The freestyle or fusion portion, where teams can do practically anything to wow the judges. The sky is the limit in freestyle."

The team watched the Kung Fu Flyers do their routine. They watched The Jumpin' Jays. As he concentrated on their amazing movements, Izzy felt an uneasiness in his stomach. He needed to gear up, but he couldn't stop watching the other performers. They all seemed so awesome, so competent. He was so used to making a big deal about his skills, but so much of it was bravado. Now he wondered: was he any good?

Apparently, Izzy wasn't the only one feeling edgy.

"Is everything ready?" Mary asked in a whisper. "Music?"

"Mary, chill out," Keisha said, "Like, technical has everything – the CD, our programme instructions."

"I just hope they get it right." Mary's hand was shaking a little.

"Would y'all calm down!" Shauna begged. "I'm trying to have a moment."

The MC announced the Dutch Dragons.

"We're right after the Dutch Dragons," Shauna said.

Izzy watched the Dragons take the stage, knowing that in a matter of minutes, that would be them. He gritted his teeth apprehensively. He clenched his jaw.

"You all right?" Mary asked.

Izzy said out loud what he'd been thinking to himself earlier.

"This is weird," he said. "I've never been on a team like this before. It used to be me and my fists. I didn't have to count on anyone else."

"You can count on us now," said Keisha.

They stood silently watching the Dutch Dragons. Izzy had to admit that Yolanda was a pill, but she was a super-smooth jumper.

"Some of these teams are really good," he remarked.

"And so are we," Keisha reminded him.

"Why are you sweating other teams?" Mary asked.

Huh? Was this the Mary who was wigging out just a few seconds ago? What had come over her?

"Whoa," said Izzy. "What did you do with Mary?"

Apparently, in the last few seconds, she'd realized that she needed to lighten up. Because she turned to him calmly and said, "Somebody told her to stop tripping and just have fun."

Of course, that somebody had been Izzy.

It was their turn.

"Let's do this!" Izzy shouted.

"Yeah! Let's do this!"

There were high fives all round.

I'm ready, Izzy told himself. He was pumped. They were seconds away from hitting the stage, when he looked into the audience. His stomach dropped as he saw his dad and sister take seats. Whoa. He even locked eyes with his dad for a second. Mr Daniels's gaze was penetrating.

The music was starting, but Izzy was paralyzed.

"Izzy!" Mary cried. She motioned to the tech booth to cut the music. She stared at Izzy as he stared at his dad. "Izzy, you can do this," she said.

Izzy thought back to the picture of him with his parents. He was so proud to be the son of a Golden Gloves winner, even if he didn't become one himself. He'd tell his dad that after this was over.

Izzy turned to Mary. She looked worried, concerned and kind all at once. He smiled gently at her, breathing in.

"I'm fine," he told her. "Let's do it."

Mary signalled to the tech booth. Music! The spotlights in the audience went black.

The MC announced them, rapping: "Put your hands up, put your hands up, everybody, put your hands up, if you're ready for the Hot Chilli Steppers to take the show somebody say 'you know!'"

The audience yelled. "You know!"

The lights went up. Mary and Shauna entered the ropes, skipping at a high speed in unison. They criss-crossed, hopscotched and kicked out over each other's heads. They grabbed the ends of the ropes from Izzy and Keisha and made a smooth transition. Now it was Izzy and Keisha's turn. The music got faster, the beat more intense.

Izzy ran from the far end of the gym and cartwheel-backflipped into the ropes. As he soared through the air, he didn't have to look to know his dad's eyes were peeled on him.

He landed in the ropes with Keisha and the crowd came to its feet.

The team did front-and-back hand claps; they even helicopter kicked. Izzy hyped the crowd.

"Go Chilli Steppers, go Chilli Steppers, go!"

The crowd called back, "Go Chilli Steppers, go Chilli Steppers, go!"

Izzy's people – his dad, his sister, Chuck,

Lil' Earl and Tammy – rose to their feet. Izzy was surprised to see Tammy there, but was glad that she'd finally seen him doing something that was *his* true passion, just as boxing was hers.

"Hold up!" Izzy yelled. "Girls, wait a minute!" Then they all screamed at once: "Let us put some soul in it!" The girls struck a pose. "Awww!" Izzy hollered. "I see you ladies. Come on everybody, clap your hands to it!"

Keisha and Shauna now turned as Mary and Izzy leapfrogged into the ropes. Mary helped Shauna do a twister, holding her hands as Keisha flipped forward. Keisha and Shauna grabbed each other by the arms, swinging each other around, feet leaving the ground like ice-skaters.

To the beat of the music, they landed on the floor, threw the ropes in the air and switched with Mary and Izzy. Izzy hunched his shoulders and remained perfectly still as he waited for Mary to jump on his shoulders. She landed, steady and light. They jumped together. Then, Mary dove off of Izzy's shoulders and somersaulted back into the ropes. Izzy fell to his stomach and did a break-dance move, which morphed into the worm. As the music came to its final strains, the Hot Chilli Steppers danced out of the ropes. The crowd cheered.

CHAPTER EIGHTEEN

The Hot Chilli Steppers reunited with their families and friends.

"Mum!" Mary yelled. "It was so much fun."

"Congratulations, baby," Mrs Thomas said. "You were wonderful."

Izzy saw Karin and his father. He felt nervous, then decided to just go for it. Karin looked positively awestruck.

"You were great," she said breathlessly.

"Thanks, Karin."

Karin scampered off to talk to the girl members of the Hot Chilli Steppers, leaving Izzy alone with his dad.

"Hey, Dad," Izzy said.

He waited for his dad to say something. Anything. The silence was deafening.

"You looked good out there," Mr Daniels said.

"Thanks," Izzy said, and then, because he was, he added: "I'm sorry."

Mr Daniels looked deeply into his son's eyes.

"No Izzy. I am. I want you to be able to talk to me about anything. After your mum died, I guess I pushed boxing even more because I thought you loved it so much and I loved it so much. It was a way to connect. To be there for each other. I love you, Izzy. I know you miss your mother, because I do, and I guess boxing was a way for me to say all that. Boxing is my dream. It doesn't have to be yours. I always said that boxing is 20 per cent talent, 80 per cent heart. Looks like your heart is somewhere else, and that's okay."

"I just wanted to be your champ," Izzy said.

"You are." They hugged. "You were great. I'm proud of you and your mum would be, too."

Just then, Chuck, Lil' Earl and Tammy ran up to them.

"Man, you were out the box!" hooted Lil' Earl.

"Off the chain," echoed Chuck.

"It's okay if you guys think it's corny," Izzy said with a shrug.

"Let's just say I've been enlightened," Chuck said. He nodded at Tammy.

Izzy grinned.

"I think I'm going to be sick," said Lil' Earl.

They were laughing when they realized they weren't alone. Rodney was coming over to talk to them. Chuck and Lil' Earl flashed Izzy a worried look.

"I got this," Izzy said.

He stood face to face with Rodney.

"I'm done fighting you, man."

"I know," said Rodney.

"So why are you here?"

"That Double Dutch thing is kinda cool . . . for a daddy's boy."

Izzy chuckled. He held out his hand to Rodney.

"Truce?" he asked.

"Yeah," said Rodney. But he had one condition. "If you teach me that flip. Maybe I can use it in the ring."

"You got it," Izzy said.

Did the Hot Chilli Steppers come first in the city regionals? No, they did not. They came second.

But next year – and there *would* be a next year, if Izzy Daniels had anything to say about it – they'd place first. And most importantly, they'd have an awesome time getting there.